To Lucy—for reminding us to find joy
in life's simple moments.

**To my husband, parents, and
grandma**—for believing in this story.

www.mascotbooks.com

SOCKS!

For more information, please contact:
Mascot Books
620 Herndon Parkway #320
Herndon, VA 20170
info@mascotbooks.com

Library of Congress Control Number: 2019912255

CPSIA Code: PRT1119A
ISBN-13: 978-1-64307-546-4

Printed in the United States

SOCKS!

Written by **Amber Morrell**

Illustrated by **Agus Prajogo**

Hi! My name is Lucy and I am a four-year-old chocolate lab.
I have a lot of favorite things: going for walks, playing in the snow,
and taking long naps.

But I want to tell you about one of my **all-time favorites**. I first discovered them in my parents' closet and they have been my thing ever since.

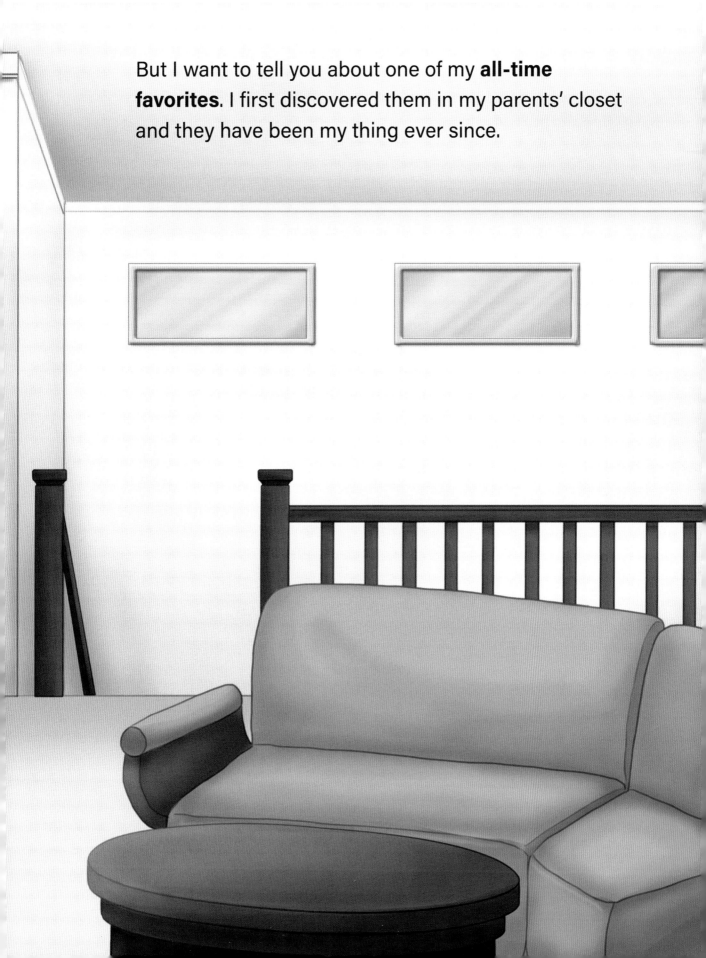

My parents have these
fancy laundry baskets they
thought I wouldn't be able
to get into.

But you know what? I could.

And I am always searching
for just one thing...

SOCKS!

Small socks, fuzzy socks, thick socks, short socks...**I LOVE SOCKS!**

I quietly walk into the closet and slide my nose under the lid of my parents' laundry basket.

I stick my head in the basket as far as it will go...

And it never fails, I find a sock!

I come out of the closet with my dirty, delicious-smelling sock. To my surprise—and delight—my parents are standing there to catch me. I freeze.

I lock eyes with them to show how proud I am of my recent find (and to make sure they acknowledge my sock). I stand as still as can be, braced and ready for the chase. This is where the fun begins!

I dash by them as fast as I can, jump up and over their bed, skid through the doorway, and bolt down the stairs with that dirty, delicious-smelling sock dangling from my jaws.

Now I have them right where I want them. They come running down the stairs shouting,

"Drop that sock, Lucy!"

I peer around the corner of the couch, just waiting to bolt in the opposite direction. As my mom and dad move toward me, I make my move.

Around and
around we go.

We spend what feels like hours running in circles before all three of us give in.

I slowly walk up to my mom and give her a nudge with that sock still hanging from my jaws.

She quickly snatches it from my mouth and takes it upstairs.

I follow her up the stairs as she tosses it right back into that fancy laundry basket—you know, the one my parents think I can't get socks out of?

And when my parents aren't looking, that's just what I do.

I slip my nose under the lid to grab a dirty, delicious-smelling sock, and come slowly walking out of the closet...

About the Author

Amber is a 2nd grade teacher in Bismarck, North Dakota. She is passionate about children's literature and her chocolate lab, Lucy. On one of the many sock chases, Amber thought, *why not tell Lucy's story?* and so *SOCKS!* unfolded. To all of those that share a passion for children's literature and their sweet pups, this book is sure to remind you of a dog's way of teaching us to find joy in life's simple moments.